Dear Parents and Educators,

Welcome to Penguin Young Readers! As parents and educators, you know that each child develops at his or her own pace—in terms of speech, critical thinking, and, of course, reading. Penguin Young Readers recognizes this fact. As a result, each Penguin Young Readers book is assigned a traditional easy-to-read level (1–4) as well as a Guided Reading Level (A–P). Both of these systems will help you choose the right book for your child. Please refer to the back of each book for specific leveling information. Penguin Young Readers features esteemed authors and illustrators, stories about favorite characters, fascinating nonfiction, and more!

The Loopy Coop Hens Letting Go	LEVEL 2
	GUIDED READING LEVEL H

This book is perfect for a **Progressing Reader** who:
- can figure out unknown words by using picture and context clues;
- can recognize beginning, middle, and ending sounds;
- can make and confirm predictions about what will happen in the text; and
- can distinguish between fiction and nonfiction.

Here are some **activities** you can do during and after reading this book:
- Problem/Solution: In this story, apples keep falling on the Loopy Coop hens. The problem is they are scared that a fox is dropping the apples. Discuss the solution to the hens' problem, and how they finally figure out why the apples are falling
- Make Connections: Pip, Midge, and Dot are terrified that a fox is in the tree. Pip and Midge refuse to go up and see. But Dot is brave and decides to climb the tree even though she is scared. At the top, she finds not a fox but a beautiful view. Have you ever faced your fears and done something even though you were scared? What happened?

Remember, sharing the love of reading with a child is the best gift you can give!

—Bonnie Bader, EdM
   Penguin Young Readers program

*Penguin Young Readers are leveled by independent reviewers applying the standards developed by Irene Fountas and Gay Su Pinnell in *Matching Books to Readers:.Using Leveled Books in Guided Reading*, Heinemann, 1999.

For Ebba—JMS

PENGUIN YOUNG READERS
Published by the Penguin Group
Penguin Group (USA) LLC, 375 Hudson Street, New York, New York 10014, USA

USA | Canada | UK | Ireland | Australia | New Zealand | India | South Africa | China

penguin.com
A Penguin Random House Company

The Library of Congress has catalogued the Dial edition under the following control number: 2012017261

ISBN 978-0-448-48458-7   10 9 8 7 6 5 4 3 2 1

The Loopy Coop Hens

Letting Go

by Janet Morgan Stoeke

Penguin Young Readers
An Imprint of Penguin Group (USA) LLC

The Tree

It is hot at Loopy Coop Farm.

Midge and Pip and Dot sit

in the shade.

"Oh!" says Midge.

"Oh!" says Pip.

"OW!" says Dot.

"Who is up there?" shouts Dot.

"Maybe it's a bird."

"Maybe it's a cat," says Pip.

"Maybe it's a FOX!" says Midge.

"Let's get out of here!"

Help

"Rooster Sam! Rooster Sam!"

they cry.

"A FOX!

He is in the tree!

He is throwing apples!"

"Come with us," say the hens.

"Please?"

Rooster Sam struts to the tree.

"Go ahead, fox!" shouts Pip.

"Throw an apple NOW!"

They wait.

Rooster Sam starts to go.

He jumps!

Then he runs!

The Ladder

"We need to go up there,"

says Dot.

"I don't like ladders,"

says Pip.

"I don't like ladders.

OR foxes," says Midge.

Click!

"I will do it," says Dot.

Dot goes way up high.

She goes to the top.

"Oh NO!" says Pip.

"Come down, Dot!"

"The fox is mad," says Midge.

"Save yourself, Dot!"

"No," says Dot.

"Come up with me.

There is no fox.

It is so pretty up here."

"But, Dot, it is not safe!" says Pip.

"Look at all these apples!

The fox threw them.

Come down."

Apple Feathers

"It is not a fox," says Dot.

"The apples just let go."

Dot shakes her wing.

"See? My feathers let go."

Dot says, "Apples let go, too.

Come on up.

You will see."

They climb the ladder

"Oops," says Midge.

"OH!" says Pip.

"You are right, Dot.

They just . . . let go."

They get to the top.

"Ooooh," says Pip.

"Ahhh," says Midge.

"I told you it was pretty," says Dot.

They look all around.

It is very pretty.

"I feel like I am an apple,"

says Pip.

"Way up high," says Dot.

"I feel like letting go."

"Me too," says Midge.

Her eyes are wide.

"Let's do it!"

"Oh!"

"Oh!"

"Whee!"

"That was fun!"

"I love being an apple!"

"Let's do it again!"